NIGHT IN THE COUNTRY

For Bob Verrone

NIGHT IN THE COUNTRY

story by CYNTHIA RYLANT

pictures by MARY SZILAGYI

BRADBURY PRESS · NEW YORK

There is no night so dark, so black as night in the country.

In little houses people lie sleeping and dreaming about
daytime things, while outside — in the fields, and by the rivers,
and deep in the trees — there is only night and nighttime
things.

There are owls. Great owls with marble eyes who swoop
among the trees and who are not afraid of night in the country.
Night birds.

There are frogs. Night frogs who sing songs for you every night:

reek reek reek reek. Night songs.

And if you are one of those people in one of those little houses, and if you cannot sleep, you will hear the sounds of night in the country all around you.

Outside, the dog's chain clinks as he gets up for a drink of water.

Far over the hill you hear someone open and close a creaking screen door. You wonder who is up so late.

And, if you lie very still, you may hear an apple
fall from the tree in the back yard.

Listen:

Pump!

Later, the rabbits will patter into your yard and eat pieces
of your fallen apples. But only when they think you are asleep.

And all around you on a night in the country
are the groans and thumps and squeaks that houses
make when they are trying, like you, to sleep.

Outside . . .

A raccoon mother licks her babies.

A cow nuzzles her calf.

An old pig rolls over in the barn.

And toward morning, one small bird will be the first to tell everyone that night in the country is nearly over.

The owls will go to sleep, the frogs will grow quiet,
the rabbits will run away.

Then they will spend a day in the country
listening to you.

Library of Congress Cataloging in Publication Data: Rylant, Cynthia. Night in the country. Summary: Text and illustrations describe the sights and sounds of nighttime in the country. [1. Night — Fiction. 2. Country life — Fiction] I. Szilagyi, Mary, ill. II. Title PZ7.R982Ni 1986 [E] 85-70963 ISBN 0-02-777210-1